Ten Ways The Animals Will Save Us

An Anthology of Flash Fictions

Edited by Gaynor Jones
Foreword by Amanda Saint

ISBN eBook: 978-1-9196087-5-4
ISBN print: 978-1-9196087-4-7

Retreat West Books
retreatwest.co.uk/books

Contents

Foreword
Amanda Saint

It seems impossible that a whole decade has passed since I first started Retreat West but somehow it has. I'm so excited to publish this celebratory anthology of flash fictions as over those ten years, flash has grown to be my favourite form to write. During that time, it has been wonderful to meet and learn from so many talented writers of flash and to see how the form has developed.

Many of the great writers I have met are featured in this anthology, alongside writers that are new to me that came through the open submission process, and I am truly grateful to all for their support of Retreat West and this book.

I am a notoriously bad record keeper so have no idea how many stories we have read and published over that decade, as to start with they were all coming in via email which was a little chaotic and hard to keep track of! But since we signed up to Submittable in 2016, we have received just under 10,000 submissions. Thank you to everyone who sends us their work – we are honoured that you trust us with it and wish we could publish more of the stories we have to decline.

For many years, I ran Retreat West all alone then in 2018, Gaynor Jones joined me to help with book promo and I am lucky that she is still with me today helping with a lot of different things. She's made it all a lot more organised and a lot more fun! Thank you, Gaynor.

Thanks also to the volunteers who read for the competitions for me: Amy Barnes, Emma Finlayson-Palmer and Joanna Campbell. I couldn't keep on top of it all without you!

And a huge thank you to all the writers who have joined our community, read our books, come on our courses and workshops, and provide regular cheering on and support on our Twitter page and by replying to our emailers with lovely messages. It's thanks to you that we have been going for ten years and hopefully will keep going for many more.

We hope you all enjoy the stories in this anthology as much as we do.

Amanda x

Ten Ways the Animals Will Save Us

Rosie Garland

1. Let's say my favourite is the tiger.
2. Let's say yours is the manatee.
3. Let's say I drop the control freak act and say how amazing, the manatee is my favourite too!
4. Let's say we go to the zoo, strip off and dive right into her pool.
5. Let's say she looks at us out of her muddy Zen eyes, smacks my shoulder with her flipper and I'm cured of the almighty stupidity I drag around and at last I can let myself love you in a way that's not broken.
6. Let's say we take the manatee home.
7. Let's say she lives in the bath.
8. Let's say she slaps sense into me every time I backslide.
9. Let's say it works: life, love, the whole damn thing.
10. Just this once, let's say I hold it together and don't let go.

Base-2

Sara Hills

When I won't let him past second base, Chris accuses me of having two settings—off and *off*. He insists I can count on him, that he can wait till I'm ready, but his eyes say different as they trail over Lucy Thompson's tight sweater and the two orange cables running racing stripe down her chest.

Lucy glides toward us through the crowded school hallway, palms out, parting the sea. She traces her gum pink fingernail across the front of Chris's math t-shirt and reads only half the words—"There are 10 types of people"—before blushing into his face. "Ten," she repeats. "Which type am I?"

Lucy's bleached teeth make straight-line pairs alongside her straight-ironed hair. She is lines upon lines, a transistor's on-switch, ten kinds of yes with a big fat zero where her brain should be.

"It's not a *ten*," I tell her, explaining the t-shirt. "It's two in binary. Like for computer coding. Duh."

Lucy ignores me like I'm not even there. She latches onto Chris's arm and begs him to tutor her in geometry, to help her finally understand the shapes of things.

Decimal ten written in binary looks like two tens butted up together—1010—and the way Chris's eyes are bouncing between us, I know he's working out the calculations in his head:

Lucy/Me. Lucy/Me = On/off. On/off.

I want to shake Chris until his eyes stop bobbling and his brain settles back into place, but my hands stay dumb at my sides and dampen, as though they're crying, as if they know I've already lost.

***

In biology class, we learn that every synapse inside the human brain is a binary switch.

On is Chris showing Lucy how to bisect an angle.

On is the narrow-eyed-look Lucy gives the quarter-back in the cafeteria.

On is a speeding train.

If a train of thought travels at 100 meters per second down Chris's neural pathways, at what point does it collide with reality?

***

Chris doesn't come to Coding Club anymore.

When the other nerds ask why we broke up, I say,

"There are 10 types of people in this world: *ones* who would give up anything to be in Lucy Thompson's proximity and *zeros* who know they don't stand a chance."

I expect our friends to laugh, to nod, to act sympathetic, but each mouth responds in a tight straight line.

Maybe Lucy's right, and I'm wrong. Maybe there are actually *ten* types of people—nine who would give up everything, and me.

I switch on my computer and run the machine code again, watching the green ones and zeros scroll across the screen, blurring, before blinking out of sight.

The Impossibility of Tin

Jan Kaneen

Paper

I use special sheets, light and thin that hold multiple folds, but it still takes a gazillion attempts to perfect the red origami heart. I put it onto your plate and lay the table to match. You text at eight—*train delayed.* I turn down the bourguignon—chosen for this very reason, because it doesn't spoil with extra cooking.

Cotton

You rip the teeny-tiny parcel open and I clock the exact nanosecond the penny drops because your eyes fill with tears. You kiss the baby socks, then me.

Leather

"Priorities change. Focuses shift. Anniversaries seem unimportant." I tell you this the week before and you look hurt. I shrug and almost smile as I feed Harry.

"Don't get me a pressie," I say, thinking – because I've already become this year's material – durable, tough, seasoned.

But when you let me lie-in and do breakfast in bed – soft-boiled eggs and toasty soldiers, give me a wristband made bespoke with the words, "Tough Mamma," I feel myself soften.

Linen

I've already fitted your gift onto the pillow when you climb into bed. You lay your head on it looking unimpressed.

"Feels cold," you say as you turn onto your side.

I hug Harry closer and face the wall.

Wood

"Any other woman would be bloody delighted," you snap.

I look at the ugly chrysanthemums that stink like sick, and think about seeing them in the service station when I filled-up earlier. When you're snoring, I go downstairs and toss them onto the dying fire along with the carved wooden love-spoon I thought you'd love, wishing I was 'any other woman'.

Sugar

The presents start coming after I drop Harry at school. A tin of posh biscuits, then expensive chocolates. At teatime, the bucket of my favourite candyfloss puts Harry on a sugar high. When you get home, I let you kiss my cheek, certain now my suspicions aren't 'all in my head.'

Wool

It takes months to finish. In the evenings after Harry's asleep. I wrap it and write a tag, *with love*, and try to mean it. I open it at midnight on our anniversary and put it on, and every time a thought of you and her slinks into my head, I chant a silent *knit one, purl one*.

Making that jumper stitched me back together, stopped me thinking, made me count every *in* and *over* and *through* and *off*.

Salt

You cry and cry, say it was a huge mistake, but you sound distant like there's a million years or miles between us and I wonder why I let you in again, tonight of all nights.

Copper

Harry looks at me, then you, then me.

"We made it together," you announce, clipping it

onto my wrist.

The sunset metal glints my initials. I smile and thank you both, but really I'm thinking what a tragedy – such a lovely dad, such a rubbish husband – and about turquoise and verdigris and things irrevocably tarnished.

'I' Statements and 'You' Statements

Monica Dickson

I

1. I know relationships can be hard work.
2. I feel like I'm being undermined.
3. I want more sex, if only we had the energy to focus on each other's needs.
4. I just didn't want a marriage like my parents' marriage.
5. I can explain. Though – frankly – I shouldn't really need to spell it out.
6. I wasn't expecting that. I mean, WOW.
7. I sometimes say stuff I don't mean when I'm angry, that's all.
8. I always have to be the one doing the emotional labour don't I?
9. I cannot put up with this for a second longer.
10. I wish you'd put us both out of our misery and leave.

You

1. You know how to turn a relationship into a full-time job.
2. You can spare me the passive-aggressive BS, I know what this is really about.
3. You must be exhausted, especially since you started having sex with someone else.
4. You think you can blame this on your daddy issues? Ha!
5. You always were a pedant.
6. You can't be serious. We've been together for 10 years and having the same pointless arguments for 9 ½ of them.
7. You have completely lost your shit on a regular basis.
8. You are the self-appointed Arbiter of Feelings. All of them, yours and mine.
9. You don't have to stay. No-one is forcing you to stay.
10. You should just put us both out of our misery and leave.

Heavy Light
Amanda Saint

The pebble weighs her down as she trudges along the beach to where she first found it. Then it was glossy and glowing, amber flecks like tiger eyes brought to life by the swish of the sea. But by the time she got home from her holiday and pulled it from her case, it was just a brown stone. She kept it though and over the years marked it for every important event. Ten gold nail varnish dots holding her most treasured memories.

She runs her fingers over the pebble in her coat pocket, seeing the moments they mark in her mind once again. First person in her family to go to uni. Honours degree, Master's degree, PhD. Her thesis turned into a bestselling book. Meeting him, marrying him, having two daughters with him. His recovery against all the odds. That final one added just two months ago.

A gull shrieks overhead and she flings her head back and screeches too, kicks at the sand. It feels so good. Screaming and stomping out all the rage she hasn't let herself show at home. She won't do that in front of their girls. Won't be the spurned wife who berates him for celebrating his survival with someone else, then begs him to stay. That is not who she is.

She reaches the end of the bay where jagged cliffs rear up to the sky. This is the place. Waves smash against the rocks, slinging spray all over her. The sea salt stings bitterly on her lips. But she likes it.

Wrenching the pebble from her pocket, she screeches again her voice bouncing back at her from the craggy cliffs. The spots of gold are dull in the heavy light. The memories that they hold are no longer gilded. The time for remembering what they shared is gone.

The slap of water on sand brings her back to the beach. Sunbeams break through chinks in the clouds, warming her face. She bends, dips the stone in the sea to make the tiger eyes appear. She needs the strength of the big cat now.

Although the wet stone glows gently, it gives her no courage. She slumps in the sand wondering whether she can carry on alone. As the incoming tide rolls towards her, she unclenches her fist. But she closes it again before the ebbing wave takes the pebble away.

She stands.

The pebble is too weighted. She has to let it go.

She takes a huge breath to fill herself with the tiger's strength and roars. With all her might, she throws the pebble as far as she can out to sea.

    As it sinks, she turns her back on it.

    So light now she could float away.

The Last Ten Seconds of Summer

Gaynor Jones

Your mother watches from the kitchen window that overlooks the sink. She always tells you to mind the hose water, that it's dirty, but in the pool you can't help but get it into your eyes, your ears. All the open places in your body.

Your friend presses you down with her foot, toes rippling in that space between the parts of your bikini top where it's just a string tied in a bow. Her wavy reflection above you mouths something that might be "close your eyes", but you leave them open, even as they sting. You look up at her. Her body is segmented by the water—thighs, midriff, shoulders—and you feel something deep, deep below your stomach. You squeeze your legs tight, try and hold onto the sensation like you try and hold onto the image of her behind your eyes after every long hot day that you're together. You're still squeezing when her foot lifts.

"That was twenty-three seconds!"

You wipe at the water spilling from your nose, check the back of your hand for streams of snot.

It is her turn to lie now. Your turn to watch.

You lean one hand on the pool for balance, and toe gently at her chest with your foot. It's electric. She pinches her nose and ducks under, but splurges upward before you even begin the count.

"Wait a minute, I just need a minute."

She breathes in, exaggerated, puffing out her stomach with each exhale.

"Okay, I'm good now."

But soon she's up again, pushing her hair back from her face. She shakes her head. Grins the grin that does to your insides what the boys' smiles do to her, to all the other girls you know.

"How long did I go?"

You forgot to count.

Her record is fourteen seconds, and she's desperate to beat it before the summer ends, before she'll swap you out for other friends, other boys, maybe even other girls, before she'll curl up her nose at the thought of playing in this cheap paddling pool, before she'll pretend not to know you, pretend that your skin never touched.

You press your hand to the centre of her chest, feel her heartbeat, start to push her back down. She looks at you, pouting, waiting for your answer. You say,

"Ten."

"Aw, man."

She kicks a little, splashing and smiling as the clouds come to steal away the sun. Your mother raps on the window, gestures at her watch. Your friend looks at you,

"Shall I keep trying?"

You nod. Watch her go down under the water. Ignore your mother. Count.

Ten of Hearts
Amanda Huggins

I sit on the sofa, you kneel on the floor at my feet. You are charming and eloquent, I am drunk and on the rebound.

"Do you believe in magic?" you ask.

I nod, curious, and you hand me a small sheet of paper from your pocket, tell me to write the name of a playing card in the centre.

You instruct me to fold the paper into a tiny square, then you press it against your forehead, hold it there with a single finger. You ask me to concentrate, to not let it out of my sight. Then you push it inside your clenched fist, drop it back into my palm.

"Your card is the ten of hearts."

I gasp. How could you possibly know?

You laugh, hold your hands up and lead me to my own bed. "It's the 10th today," you say, "and you've stolen my heart."

In the morning you kiss me gently before you break the spell, before you explain about sleight of hand and misdirection, how the paper you pressed against your forehead was a blank sheet, folded earlier. You'd already dropped my square to the floor, unfolded it with your free hand under the edge of the sofa; then you read it, re-folded it, palmed it, slipped it back into my hand.

You say I'm bound to you forever now, entrusted with one of magic's sacred secrets.

A week later, you move in. We become a double act, performing in every pub for miles around, arriving late when the crowd are unsteady on their feet. Drunken mouths hang agape as lit cigarettes vanish inside your tightly clenched fist never to be seen again. You stake your fake Rolex on a three-card trick, win the punter's confidence and his genuine Omega, produce banknotes from beneath table legs, coins from behind gullible ears. Every time you ask a punter to choose a card they choose the ten of hearts, and you look at me, smile and wink. We steal earrings and bracelets off the earlobes and wrists of the misdirected, slip out into the night with their angry shouts echoing down the street.

You say everything is hotting up, that we need to drive further afield, to sprinkle our magic over a new city. You persuade me to take out a car loan for an Audi which you register in your name.

Things disappear the night after you collect that gleaming black machine: my watch, my diamond earrings and my debit card, £200 in cash, the lucky ten of hearts I kept safe beneath my pillow. When I challenge you, you act affronted, twist my words back on me, then carry your suitcases to the car.

When I go over to the window and watch you drive away, I find the ten of hearts blu-tacked to the glass. That's when I hear your voice in my head, telling me that magic is nothing more than a set of cheap tricks.

Ten Ways To Prepare For Your Brothers' Visit

Jude Higgins

1. Window sills. Remove your wedding pictures and replace with childhood family snaps.
2. Garden. Pick the rotting apples from the tree your ex-husband gave you years ago. Variety – 'Allen's Everlasting.' When your brothers arrive, you'll point out the charm of goldfinches feeding on evening primrose seeds. They won't see the parliament of rooks in the ash tree, or hear their harsh calls repeating you're not entitled to benefits.
3. Kitchen. Remove tannin stains from the teacups. Your brothers have dishwashers to create a sparkle. (You'd put your whole life in a dishwasher if you owned one).
4. Bathroom. Brush your teeth with whitening toothpaste. You'll need to smile. Sweep the doctor's tablets out of the cabinet into the back of a drawer in case anyone snoops.
5. Living room. Burn orange-perfumed essential oil to dispel the stale smell of cigarettes and create a positive

atmosphere. Move the remaining furniture around so the room looks less bare.

6. Hall. Get down on your knees and scrub the tiles. Twenty years of couple grime is hard to remove. That's not something an ex-husband wants to take with him.

7. Bedroom. Study your dishevelled appearance in the long mirror. Tie your hair back. Change your clothes three times. No black – you've read it makes the older woman's skin pale to insignificance. Settle on the red cashmere. Lipstick. A bright scarf. When they're driving home, you want your brothers and their wives to agree you 'don't look too bad, all things considered.'

8. Dining Room. Lay out the bread, cold cuts, olives, cheeses and deli pastries on the tablecloth embroidered by your mother. (Talking point). Arrange a posy of nasturtiums at the centre of the table. Open the last bottle of good Rioja. Play 'A Kind of Blue', the album you and your husband both used to like.

9. Easy Chair. Relax—you can do this.

10. When brother one rings up to say something's come up at work and brother two says sorry it's so late but his wife forgot an important church function, slump on the sofa and cry.

Forging the Links
Christine Collinson

The Black Country, 1910

I began making chains as a mere rod of a girl. My young hands, soft and pliable, worked the glowing links from sunup to twilight. Youthful muscles, not broad enough then to pump the bellows as now. After, Ma dunked us, me, and my sisters. She doused our smoky hair. "I'll never wash the forge out of you girls!" she'd laughed. I'd scrubbed my nails and held them up for inspection as the water deepened to night.

And now I have my chance, my time. The call to strike for fair wages is uniting us, women one and all. Our voices are finding strength. My roughened hands are idle for the first time in years, my hair is slick with rain. The soles of my boots aren't thick with ash, but puddle drenched. We sing as we walk home from the meeting hall. Striding side-by-side, elbows joined, it's like nothing will ever be as before. My voice adds to the echo of our rallying song, my laughter alloys with theirs.

The village air is clearer without the forge fires. When Ma hung out the laundry all those days ago, I'd watch it swing in the breeze like sails. "While the wind blows the other way, the linens won't stink!" she'd grin, tucking unruly hair beneath her cap. "You can fetch it in, Bessie, it's your turn." It always seemed to be my turn. I was the eldest, trying to help my sisters learn.

Behind Ma's smile lay burden. I see that now more plainly. Of day-long toil, of trying to keep the hearth bright in winter, of filling our plates enough to quell simmering hunger. Pa, up at the town forge from dawn to sundown, we barely saw. I'd glance at the low-lit lines of his face, see the rawness of his palms; he was all sinew and bone. He seemed sturdy to me, as solid as the iron we all knew so well, but eventually he weakened, and was gone. Ten winters ago, ten years of memories alone. And then Ma, beaten down to a whisper of herself, left us too.

Pausing in the doorway of our empty forge, I check that all is well for the night. Hear the clink-clink of hammers, the puff of the bellows, boot-heels over stone. Absorbed by the absence of it, listen only to the wind murmuring down the cold chimney.

We've marched on a path untrodden; women of the forges out on the streets, so many of us, together. The song in my heart is pounding louder. If we persist, if we can win, new links in the chains can start. The coin I dream of in my work-heavy hands would weigh like nuggets of gold.

The World's Best Daughter
Michael Loveday

Ten thousand doors, opening and closing in succession – and through those doors, ten thousand worlds I must abandon as I greet them. I screw my mind into the task. My hand is callused, ankles weak, calves cramped and burning.

Father readies his whistle, looks at his watch. A pause for prayer, offered to that God who oversees our cause: He has the power to break the thread of our pulse at any moment of His choosing. Then, one shrill blast and I begin.

I grasp the handle, push until the black door gives, step through, then close the door behind. *Turn!* my father cries. I face the same door's white reverse, drag it open, cross and stand exactly where I stood before. *Turn!* he cries, again.

Over the fence, our neighbour watches: "Fools!" He spits and walks away.

My father built this door soon after I was born. Painted one side black, one white. In a clearing in our small orchard, he fixed its frame into the dirt. *May no wind rip it down, however wild.* And now, each dawn, I rise and go into the garden. *You'll be the bloom upon our nation's soil.* My father calls from where he waits amongst the trees.

The door has taught me its moods. I am a dancer in a ballet. And at the ceremony's heart, an older emptiness. Our tale is one of earth-poor farmers, reaching hard into the past. *Dream your giant dreams tonight, my love! Soon, you'll free the shackles our family has worn for many years.*

My calling is to learn about the door, its creaks, its swings, its whims of mild resistance. At night, I pick the splinters from my hands until, exhausted, my body plummets into darkness.

I am the fittest of the village children now. Black-white, black-white, repeat – I'll cross more thresholds than anyone before me! Glory will surely come, father says, once the world hears of my feats. Our nation's leader – blessed President! God's envoy! – has offered a great reward.

Lunch, 12:15, 10 March
Martha Lane

1999

In a lunchbox that he picked himself, shiny and red. A chunky navy clip on top. A lion on the front, spiky mane shooting out lightening bolts. Ham sandwiches thick with butter, crusts off because that's how Mum knows he likes them. A chocolate bar wrapped in blackcurrant purple. Crisps, raisins, a bright apple the colour of grass, yoghurt, and juice.

2001

Still guarded by the lion, stickers fraying. Bread and butter, crusts on. The apple bruised. Cheese that's waxy and flavourless. There hasn't been a biscuit since Mum.

2002

A sandwich bag full of dry cereal. Sticks in his throat like sawdust.

2003

On a white tray, divided into sections to stop the gravy and custard merging like a muddy river pouring into the sea. Lumpy mashed potatoes, salty breaded lamb cutlet, mint sauce stinging with vinegar, chocolate sponge. The free school meal kids ushered to the front of the queue. Everyone knows why they line up first. He eats staring at his untied trainers.

2004

A bag of crisps, two chocolate bars and chewing gum. Nicked from the till in the corner shop. He wasn't standing in that fucking dinner queue again.

2007

Beans on toast. Real butter, yellow like pollen. Seconds. Thirds if he wants them. Fags confiscated at the door and a promise they'd find a proper bag for him before he left. A king-size lion bar and sugary tea for pudding. Sarah watching his every mouthful, tells him to help himself to anything during his stay.

2009

Fish and chips, greasy and hot. Jackie paid. He always does after a job. First few times the adrenaline made everything taste like ash. Not now. Doesn't matter how much gear's been shifted, the batter tastes good, soggy with curry sauce. Washed down with something fizzy. Jackie jokes through a gappy grin, "those drinks'll make your teeth fall out."

2012

Tasteless, colourless. Nothing more than fuel. Surviving rather than thriving. Crammed on a long table that doesn't have enough room for the grey-sweatshirt men sitting at it. Eaten with plastic cutlery because none of them are trusted.

2015

Chocolate Digestives, dunked. Two. Tea only half-finished. Lacking the stomach for anything more. Mum's cool fingers outstretched over the table, asking for forgiveness. He says yes. Means something else. Something that can't be said in one word, one syllable. Something that tastes like undercooked rice, chalky, sticks between his teeth.

2019

Hotdogs. Supervised. Rehearsed. Frankfurters for the kids. Lincolnshire, specked with black pepper and sage, for him. Sauces and caramelised onions already laid out. Stirred slowly with butter, water, olive oil and thyme. The way Sarah taught him. He builds their food in front of them, loading the finger buns comically high. Sweet mustard giggles scent the room as ketchup stains his nose. He wipes it clean, hopes he can keep it that way.

Mrs Carmichael won't be happy when we get back because (1) we'll be late and (2) the kids will be hyper on the blackcurrant lollies we'll have used as a bribe to keep them quiet and (3) there'll be the need for parental phone calls and (4) the governors will have questions about whether the risk assessment was correctly carried out

Matt Kendrick

But in this moment, in the clearing by the large oak where we've been practising survival skills, the spectre of Mrs Carmichael hasn't yet entered our collective psyche, us three teachers, in the flustered post-register phase of trying to realign a basic construct of mathematical thought. The number after nine is now eleven. Four plus six is eleven. Two times five is eleven. There are eleven pins at the end of a bowling alley and, somehow, they still arrange themselves neatly into a triangle.

Come on children, let's try it, shall we?

They seem to sense the importance of complying with our wishes and get right to it.

Very good.

We pat them on the head as we count one, two, three, four, five, six, seven, eight, nine, eleven. Freddy H has nits – we try to convince ourselves that's why we skip him out.

Eleven children, three teachers, all of us just waiting on Mr Jeavons who's off on a treasure hunt for yo-yos and second-hand pullovers. Also, footprints. He's taking longer than expected – which is bad because Charlie K is starting to annoy us with his wandering into the bushes, raising his hand to make pedantic statements of fact.

To fill the void, we suggest Eleven Green Bottles Hanging on the Wall. But not you Freddy H because you've got to rest your voice for the school pantomime where you're playing a talking tree. And you others, let's not do the falling down because we've had enough excitement for one day, haven't we? Instead, those eleven green bottles are going to hang on the wall without incident through eleven identical verses.

Mr Jeavons just needs more time.

But still Charlie K's hand shoots up. It shoots up because he's eight and that's what eight-year-old hands are wont to do. It shoots up because he's enthusiastic, energetic, unrelenting. It shoots up because he's the eleventh plague of God-damned Egypt.

What is it, Charlie?

It's just you did tell us we should find a good hiding place. And the abandoned bunker is the best place there is. I wish I'd found it. What does Freddy H win for surviving so long in the woods?

We say, Nothing.

We try to smile but our smiles are ELEVENse and tight. Sweat glisELEVENs on our skin even though the heat of the day is over and we should've been stuck in traffic by now somewhere on the A456 between Mamble and ELEVENbury Wells. Maybe we should phone Mrs Carmichael and tell her we're going to be late. But here finally is Mr Jeavons and, thank goodness, he's walking in a shepherding kind of way.

Freddy H, where have you been? No, there's no time for excuses. Let's just count everyone then get back to the bus. Form a triangle like we've practised. One, two, three, four, five, six, seven, eight, nine, eleven.

We sigh.

Charlie K really is the eleventh plague of Egypt – we try to convince ourselves that's why we skip him out.

Ten Bellies

Rebecca Field

At high school, her nickname was ten bellies. Annelise told her mother she'd won an impromptu eating contest in the canteen, wolfing down more hot dogs than anyone else. There was a kernel of truth in this lie.

The truth was that Annelise's appetite was insatiable.

But it hadn't started out that way. When Philip joined the school she thought he was all she'd ever want. She consumed him regularly; on the lane behind the tennis courts in free periods, in the back of his car with the radio blaring, in the local nightclub on a Saturday night. But when she caught him with her friend Donna at the back of the school bus, she felt sick. She barely ate a thing for a week.

She met Alan, James and Callum at various teenage house parties over the summer, devouring them whole; in the locked bathroom while others banged at the door, in a parental bedroom (watched by a salivating German Shepherd), and in a summer house at the bottom of a garden, piece by satisfying piece.

Soon her reputation preceded her. The men exchanged glances as she entered the room, licked their lips, joked about who might be next. She made short work of Lucas after he got off at her bus stop, offered to walk her home. She gulped him down in large meaty pieces, savoured the taste of him, lingering over his fingers, hiding one under her pillow for later.

Steven and Greg followed in quick succession. She got a bit careless after one night on the tiles, had to hide Greg in the pantry when her mother came down to ask what all the noise was. "If you're hungry, I don't mind rustling you up a quick omelette," she said, making herself a mug of Horlicks and padding back upstairs in her camel-coloured dressing gown.

When Annelise met Gary in the local pub, she hungered for him in a way she'd never felt before. His huge frame dominated the room; Annelise couldn't wait to get her hands onto his fleshy thighs, to squeeze his belly fat between her fingers. They sized each other up over pints of beer, Annelise gulping down a pack of dry-roasted peanuts as Gary threw darts with the lads. After closing time they gravitated to an alleyway behind the nightclub, no witnesses except for the CCTV cameras, which only added to their thrill. It was a frenzied encounter; teeth clashing, fingers grasping, passions colliding.

The next morning the nightclub cleaner swept aside

the bones, intertwined like kindling. She picked up the torn clothing that lay amongst the broken bottles and takeaway cartons, swilled the gristly remnants of their feast down the drain with a bucket of soapy water. In the corner she found a handbag and a wallet, dusted them down and went home happy.

Ten things you know about hooded crows

Ruth Brandt

1. Er, they're black and grey.
2. Dark, feathery and loud.
3. And, being crows, they keep themselves to themselves. Not like your rook who's part of a social group. A rookery of rooks which swoops around treetops at twilight, cawing and gawping at you as you stand outside your house in your bare feet.
4. People, that is people who know nothing about hooded crows, think that go-it-alone birds wouldn't mock you as you stand in your garden in your bare feet in the swamped evening mist, afraid to go back inside.
5. Doh, they have hoods. Blindingly obvious really now that you think about it. It's in the name. They're inherently concealed. And having got to five, you realise five things is a lot to know about something you've avoided thinking about till now.
6. Just an individual. Not part of a gang, which could be

scary. So how come you're outside, with no shoes or coat, and it's inside? Outside with a bag that contains nothing like shoes or a coat, but instead has a book you've never read and a melted sweet that you only know is there because it stuck to your fingers when you shoved in a handful of knickers, all the clothes you grabbed.

7. More of a daytime bird, your hooded crow. It pecks at lawns in bright sunshine, perches on branches, hangs out, not doing a lot. Almost majestic, your lone hooded crow is. Worth taking a look at, a real stare, because your hooded crow really likes turning heads. Look at me, it says as you wander past. Look at me, because if you admire me I may, just may, turn my attention to you, and you'll really like my attention. Oh yes, you will.

8. And once you're enchanted by your hooded crow – not a regular crow mind and certainly not a rook, because team players seem to take against your hooded crow – once you're enchanted by this bird that once glanced at you sideways with a respectful nod, so enchanted that you've given up friends and work for it, even given up leaving your house for fear it will fly away if you're not there to adore it, only then will it release its dollops of shit and head off anyway, returning with a feather out of place, a dark squawk, and always a peck peck peck.

9. Only then do you realise this thing. Your hooded crow has wings, but you have legs and feet, and even bare feet can walk, even when you're iced all the way to the bones by the crepuscular mist.

10. It's surprising how much you find you actually know about hooded crows. And now you've listed them out, it's clear you'll recognise one in future. And when you do, you'll instantly know to steer well clear of numbers 2-9. Easy. That's the final and best thing to know about hooded crows.

All for One, And Then There Were None

Mandira Pattnaik

Dad scrambles to make ten shadow figures in ten minutes. His ombromanie show is called Magic Digits. We watch intently as fingers make a fawn, hased by a hyena, a barking wolf. Predator and prey. Howling, hounding, escaping.

Lastly, both palms join to imitate flapping wings, flamingoes in flight.

My fingers are rolled into a fist while the rest of the class clap.

At lunch, Martha gapes at my three fingers, thrust inches from her nose.

"Kissed a-a-ll of them?"

"Yup", my lie makes me cool in a place I don't belong. My father is a tycoon to my new fourth grade class, I'm heir to my grandma's manor up in the Swiss mountains.

That evening, in a shabby dark corner of our one-room apartment, my cheek burns when five of my father's fingers make a concerted sharp slice across my face. He returns to mash the fufu, his knuckles in perfect synchrony. I try again. Close, then unfurl my fingers, one by one, starting from the littlest. Count again.

"Two, Dad. Two birds remaining," wishing none of the birds sitting on the tree in my arithmetic problem never did fly away at all.

A Small Window of Time
Natalia Snider

Listen, because that is part of solving the problem: An old man takes a flight leaving at 6:55pm departing from 32°N and, 96°W. As the plane ascends, he finds himself in the extension of the evening light; in a suspension of visual bliss; in a sunset that doesn't set.

He didn't know it was possible to exist inside a fleeting moment. To live parallel to such an explosion of colour and light. Mesmerized at the small oval window he forgets his pain. The colours remind him of his son and the feeling he felt when he was born.

The ERJ 175 reaches a cruising altitude of 33,000 feet, and he sees green where the blue horizon meets melting yellow; an impossible hue for the sky. He thinks how proud he is of who his son has become, warmth filling his heart through his eyes.

The plane moves across pillows of clouds, pink on bottom and white on top. He has never seen a cloud from every perspective like this before. His son is married now with his own children. Grandchildren.

The horizon splits with the fiery orb of the sun crossing the Gulf of Mexico. He sees sapphire in the deep sky above, indigo in the vast ocean below, and the sunsets rainbow banding in the centre. The old man thinks of his grandchildren's faces and what age they must be now.

He recognizes that closest to the sun, each colour's lines are tight and focused, each hue separate from the next. On the East side, he sees the stripes are broad, fading into the next with no finite ending or beginning to the colours. He remembers the fight but can't grasp its importance anymore. He recalls how long it's been since he's seen his family. Since he's spoken to his son. He considers the extension of time and living a whole life within glimpses and fragments.

He wonders if one would get bored of bliss and contentment.

But he thinks this sunset flight is the best-kept secret in the world and wants to share it with someone. Show them that something extraordinary can last if you just have the right algorithm.

The plane gradually decreases in speed 32 minutes before its ETA in preparation for landing. The sky gives way to a darker hue, and the lights illuminate the city below. A scene he has seen a hundred times. One he used to find pleasure in, but now he feels jaded from the brilliance past. He watches the flicker of uneasy streetlights in the industrial area near the landing strip. The abandoned parking lots and empty warehouses lit for no one and nothing to live in, yet it reminds him of home. The landing is jarring even when expected. He turns his phone on, it blinks the 10th of October, and waits for a message that never comes.

Caring for Your Dad – Ten Top Tips

Chris Cottom

1. Choose a Dad with established roots. A Dad from good stock will thrive in all conditions.
2. A new Dad should be well watered.
3. To see your Dad blossom, plant him in front of a road atlas and Primus stove.
4. Dads require little maintenance. Just fertilise yours occasionally with a pint of beer. All Dads dethatch naturally.
5. Leggy seedlings in ears, eyebrows and nostrils should be dug out, rather than pruned. Virulent growth on older specimens is extremely unsightly.
6. At the first frost, wrap your Dad in a shapeless cardigan of indeterminate colour and vintage, and leave until spring.
7. Left untended, your Dad will develop a tilth of crumbs, cigarette ash, dandruff and bogies. This is perfectly normal.
8. If you hear your Dad chuntering about Bobby

Charlton or miles per gallon, you have an outbreak of Boring Dad Blight and should apply a pair of headphones.

9. At Christmas, your Dad can be forgotten, although some owners like to decorate theirs with handkerchiefs and socks.

10. After 14 years, you will find your Dad has outlived his usefulness and can be left to mulch in a quiet corner of the lounge.

Alive

Philip Charter

It was weeks before you freed the guitar from its case. You breathe the wood-oil smell and explore the contours for imperfections, sailing a finger over the sunburst finish. Hold a note. Imagine the sustain.

Jeremy hates it when you go through his father's things, especially the guitar. Teenagers don't put their memories on display. They keep them locked away with never-spoken words. The *brak-brak-brak* of an on-screen battle rages in his bedroom. He doesn't know that Adam named him after a song on Pearl Jam's perfect debut album, *Ten*. You decided against the music for the funeral. Lyrics that held you together now tear you apart.

One night, overflowing with swallowed tears and nineties nostalgia, you opened the guitar case and vowed to learn. They say you should master the basics—spidery scales and chords to strengthen withered hands—but you went straight for tutorials on the band's top ten riffs. Every day you rehearsed, unplugged and in secret. Your fingers grew calluses and when you picked them off, they grew back thicker. As you ghost the shapes and patterns on the neck, his hands close over yours, and each night, your grief goes to sleep in the case.

When *Ten* hit the charts, he was Jeremy's age, waiting for the birth of Grunge, even if he didn't know it. Adam never got past his long-hair-baggy-cap phase, even when the office quietly suggested he adopt a professional look. Decades later, you trigger the album playlist, over and over. *Brak-brak-brak*. Was it playing when he crashed? You can't remember where they took the van's shattered carcass.

A few more weeks, months, of practice. Seasons pass. The ritual. Cradle the Les Paul, explore the contours, breathe the barely-there smell, warm your hands on the sunburst. Hold the note. Sustain. Endure.

Imagine it plugged in. You dial the amp to that signature distortion-buzz. Like anti-sound, it kills the noise in your head. The riff will soar; it will puncture the walls and deaden the gunshots ringing in Jeremy's ears. He'll cast off his headphones and join you in the living room. He'll listen to the unison of parental hands and the notes which bathe the house in the sounds of *Alive*. He knows the words by heart.

Stairs

Ian O'Brien

The tenth always creaked. When I was small and you carried me to bed, you'd mean to miss it but always forgot and I would count, pretend to be asleep, wait for the creak, suppress a laugh when you swore beneath your breath. I'd pretend to wake then, stir and ask for a story. I'd let you feel it was your fault, miscounting the tenth and waking me. And you'd tell me stories your own Mum told you: Rapunzel, Midas, spin a gold web.

When Baby Jack was born, I waited on the stairs. Your room was out of bounds and I watched the fixed blank face of the door and heard your cries swell the room. The woman from over the road kept coming out, florid, heaved up and down the stairs with water, towels, never letting go of the rosary. She made as if to ruffle my hair, stopped herself, her heavy step creaking on the tenth, the groan from the wood pained, indignant. I remember the sound of Baby Jack's first cry and the relieved cooing of the woman and I was already jealous. For that brief time he was alive and I was second best, I stood and squeezed my weight onto the stair, forcing it to creak, my weight unable to make it groan the way that she had, it sounded thin, a laugh.

Years later and I am waiting for the doctor to come out of the quiet room. I wait on the stairs, pick at yellow thread, listen to the rosary. The doctor will not emerge for another hour and when he does I will stand and go in, without reading his face. I sit on the twelfth, my feet on the ninth. I'll stand stiffly, hold the rail. I will skip the tenth completely, as if knowing that just the sound of it will not let me bear its weight.

The Running Resolution

FJ Morris

— Start-line / JD Sports —

It will be the last time. He won't do it again with Lewis,
no matter how desperate.

Jacob holds the shop in the corner of his eye as if it might
pounce.

Music blares.

Runners stretch.

He clocks everyone's shoes: Hokas, Brookes, and Nikes.

The crowd edges forward. Sardines. Bit by bit.

When Jacob crosses the start line, he already feels behind.

— 1km —

The key is to pace yourself. Don't start too fast.

Jacob also found this to be true with food when he was
starving.

— 2km / B&Q —

His Mum bought gaffer tape here.

She used it to hold his second-hand running shoes together.

Kids called him McGaffer.

But the shoes lasted another two months.

— 3km / Oakbridge Primary —

The first time he met Lewis, he was six. Lewis had excellent canines and a shaved head and was the only one who saw Jacob had no lunch that day, so shared his.

— 4km / Local Londis —

The first time they took without paying, Lewis' nostrils flared. They grabbed a Lion bar from the shelf, snuck it into their pockets, and ran into the rain, roaring as they went.

— 5km —

This is where you can make strides to get ahead.

The pack start to wane.

Jacob's weight and height become an advantage, but his sins are sticking in his sinuses.

And he hears his mum's whispers with every step:

sorry,

sorry,

sorry.

— At 6km / His street —

This is where it hurts.

When he came home with milk and no receipt, his mum pushed him to his knees, and kissed his head, and told him to say sorry a hundred times to the Almighty, to the Lamb of God.

With every sip she took she whispered *sorrysorrysorry*,

and now he wonders how many it would take for him to be forgiven this time,

so that he could breathe, so he could win.

— 7km / Red Lion pub —

Lewis said it was *eat or be eaten*. The real predators were higher up.

He took what was rightfully his, restoring God's justice to earth.

— 8km / Our Lady of Sorrows —

When the donation tray goes around, his mother gives their money away every Sunday, to the church. She says it's for the needy. But Jacob doesn't understand why the Deacon needs to have shiny-white PUMAS when he doesn't even run.

— 9km —

He feels that he's running slow, heavy.

He used to blame his shoes; his old, holy shoes.

But nobody is in front of him.

He sees the ribbon.

He hears the cheers.

His name is being called.

He looks down at his bright white Hoka shoes;

the ones he'd taken because the cloud-like soles look like heaven,

because he hoped he'd run as if blessed.

Because maybe Lewis was right.

Maybe this was justice.

Because Jacob is the first to cross the line.

— 10km —

A Sacred Number
Edward Barnfield

The first thing that hits you is the smell. Old food and rising damp, yellow books and dried mud in the carpet.

Danny is almost always on the sofa, either asleep or hunched over a battered laptop, stabbing at the keyboard like he hates it. Milo, his aging black Lab, will be at his feet. You always wonder who the biggest contributor to the mess is.

"Hey, Danny," you say, "How's it going?" It was and remains a futile question.

He gave you a key a few months back, ostensibly so you could look in on Milo, but you suspect there was a different motive, another anticipated outcome. A canine sniffing at a slumped form. A friendly acquaintance to inform the police.

"Excellent. Progress," he'll say, or "Stuck. Lost in the equations," and he'll direct you to a chair covered in mathematics texts. The odds are good there'll be an empty bottle stuffed behind the cushion beneath you.

These visits have become a Sunday habit, a regular pilgrimage. Suzie used to come, made herself busy with washing up or indoor refuse collection, but she won't anymore. "He's too angry," she says. "He doesn't want me there."

You want to make her understand that this is just a bad patch, that your mutual friend – who gave such a beautiful speech at your wedding – has endured a series of setbacks and is recuperating, recovering, the way human beings have always needed to do.

Or perhaps you retreat further into history, to the time before her, when Danny was the brightest shine of your school years, a boy destined for distinction. You could talk about the excitement of his first book, 'Acousmatics,' a popular science success that rethought Pythagoras for the 21st century, his radio appearances, the tour.

You want to say all that, but your arguments falter at the state of the kitchen, the underfed dog. You wonder if you're just trying to justify your own choices; to understand what it means that your oldest associate, the smartest person in your life, has fallen so far.

"Pythagoras declared that ten was the most sacred number. The key to the world," he says, eyes red, something sour on his breath. "Existence, creation, life, and the four elements. $1 + 2 + 3 + 4 = 10$. Everything you need."

You take heart at this. Conversations around the hypotenuse, the properties of dodecahedrons, the cult of numbers, are always more manageable than rants about the coldness of children, the malice of his ex. Even now, mathematics offers the illusion of structure, you hope.

"Only," he says, "we need more than that these days, don't we? You have to factor in family, career. Legacy. Good television."

You smile, wondering if, at this late stage, your friend has finally developed a sense of humour. Then you realise he's crying.

"That's the problem with the world," he says. "The numbers don't add up."

The Drop
Tom O'Brien

One

He'd been counting the seconds since lightning hit the tower block where he lived, miles across the city. He could see it from his desk; the two buildings like poles of a magnet.

The counting was something he'd done since a boy. His father told him, before he disappeared, that there was magic in the time between lightning and its thunder.

Two

No one else on his floor had noticed the flash, not even Elle. Their eyes were fixed on screens, or that nowhere place where a phone call happens. Around them the indoor weather of tapping keyboards, drifting conversations and occasional guffaws, rumbled on.

Owen lifted his finger off the mouse and stood.

Three

The room-high windows stood between pillars deep enough for workers to step into, leaving only their voices behind as they danced to the joyless music of a ringing phone.

Owen stared at the building he'd left this morning. Lena would be awake now. Had she felt the bolt hit their home?

He looked down to the rain-glossed street. From above it looked glamorous, urbane, energising. This morning it had been a journey through grey canyons.

Four

The swell of a transparent umbrella moved through the black ones but he couldn't identify the shape underneath.

Five

Some days the striplights reflected on glass made for impossible worlds above the cityscape. Pillars of light between high rise and gothic spires, the tail lights of an escaping plane across the office ceiling. He'd shown Lena pictures on his phone, but she didn't see what he saw, only what was there, and asked who everyone was.

Six

No reflections today. A single raindrop hung suspended in the window frame, as if on air.

Owen leaned close to the swollen bead, pregnant with the city inside, hung over the sky, perfect and inverted.

He wanted to touch it, but knew if he could, if he did, it would shatter.

Seven

Elle appeared beside him, her scent like fresh rain. Owen's stomach fell. They'd agreed; not at work, yet.

"So, what are we looking at?" she asked, close as a kiss, her breath brushed the silent question against his cheek.

He moved from her. He'd done as she asked. She could wait.

Eight

"This," he said, pointing to the optical illusion. "Looks impossible."

She leaned in and he shifted again, reaching out to steady himself against the glass but there was none. The frame was empty; no glass, no resistance, no support.

Owen toppled forward, outward, down.

Nine

Twisting, he grabbed at what was already out of reach.

Through the terminal wind Elle said, "Oh," but she was reacting to him crashing through the raindrop he'd destroyed.

Ten

By the time she screamed, from her belly, Owen's colours mixed with street rain.

Thunder from lightning ten miles away drowned her cry.

Fishing for Green and Blue
Judy Darley

Yara lowers the hook into the murky water. The greenish blue shape is beyond her reach. She wriggles closer on her belly.

It looks like a mass of jellyfish, but anyone knows that things resembling sea creatures are almost always plastic.

With one more lunge, she snares the clump and drags up her catch.

The treasure is a tangle of ten single-use masks – each one a brilliant turquoise.

They must date back a decade.

Ten is Yara's lucky number, latched to a fuzzy memory of her mother tapping each of her fingers and toes while singing some nursery rhyme, back when the world still felt safe.

Yara thinks of the refugee camp she lived in when she first came to the UK. At the edge of the camp stood a single damson tree marking seasons with white flowers and indigo fruit.

That was before the rest of the population learnt the bruised feeling of being displaced by rising seas.

She races through the Cornish survivors' territory lashed together from polyurethane and polystyrene. The ground rises and falls beneath her thudding heels. A goat bleats as she passes and releases a stream of pellets that will become fertiliser.

Georgia sailed in by catamaran after London sank four years ago. Yara was just ten then. Georgia rebuilt Yara's hut more sturdily and moved in. The relief of having someone full grown beside her rippled through Yara every night for weeks.

Now, Georgia's snoozing outside the hut, a ragged sunhat over her face. Yara kneels and tickles bare toes until she has to dodge kicking feet.

"Ah, what?" Georgia snorts. Her words stink of fermented seaweed.

"Can I borrow the Cat?" Yara asks. "You can come too."

"Ah, why not?"

Georgia strides to the boat, hat held to her head as though a gale blows. The way she swings her free arm suggests a larger, more imposing frame than hers.

The boat is as broad as a small territory itself. Yara has embellished the mainsail with vivid scraps trimmed into decagons.

Yara leans over the sides, searching for any flashes that

might glimmer up. She's so focused on the sea that she doesn't see the small island bobbing closer until Georgia yells, "Land ho!"

Like their own, it looks entirely formed from discarded plastic packaging and countless flipflops.

One difference turns Yara's breath quick and shallow.

The tree stands taller than her, quivering with green flags. Dusky purple baubles hang almost within reach.

***

Yara unrolls the catamaran sail to reveal a decagon patchwork as multi-coloured as the platform they float on. Above these, she's appliquéd leaves shaped from the medical masks. They wave in the breeze – part tree, part sky.

Georgia removes the straw hat, screwing up her eyes and beaming.

The smaller island drifts towards the horizon, green flags aflutter. Yara's pockets brim with ten damsons. In her mind, the stones at their hearts glow with life waiting to happen.

The President's Tenth Concubine
Reshma Ruia

The first time I met the President, I was ten. I was still in junior school, a chit of a girl with pigtails and a pink lace frock. The President came to our school and gave a speech about unity and independence. On his way out, he tweaked my cheek and said I was cute. The next time I saw him, I was twenty, a student at Makerere University in Kampala, walking to the library, arm in arm with my best friend Joy. A Mercedes—long and lean like a silver crocodile overtook us. It drove slowly and vanished around the bend. We thought nothing of it. The car did a U-turn and came towards us. Tinted windows and a purring engine, soft and quiet. The car stopped, a window rolled down on the driver's side. Two fat fingers beckoned us over. We walked to the car.

"What do you want?" Joy asked.

"Not you. It's she. The little pretty one he want," the driver said, jutting his chin towards the back of the car. We made out a shadowy figure of a large man sitting in traditional robes. The gold chains around his neck glinted in the darkness of the car.

He flicked out his tongue and ran them over his lips.

Joy whispered to me. "You be careful. You don't be falling into any trap."

I was naïve and innocent like a waterfall. I felt flattered that someone important wanted to be with me. I opened the car door and slid inside.

It was the President. "Come closer girl," he said. His voice was a low growl.

I did as I was told. He took my hand and pressed it against his chest. "I remember you. It was ten years back. You wore a pink lace frock."

His diamond rings grazed my skin but I was speechless. What could I say? This was the father of the nation our President.

"I will call you my Tinkerbell," he said.

The car swept into the Presidential palace that stood outside the city on the big, dusty hill.

"Some fine French champagne for this fine young lady," he ordered the ten khaki uniformed soldiers who saluted him as we went inside.

Marble floors, crystal chandeliers. Even a peacock that roamed through the rooms. Rarely had I seen such wealth. I wanted to run back home and tell my parents.

"Now you be going upstairs to the bedroom and change. I have a wardrobe full of Italian dresses. Get rid of the rags you're wearing." He clapped his hands and a stern looking woman appeared. She had thin lips and a green mole on her chin.

"Jane, you please take Tinkerbell upstairs. Get her washed and powdered and ready for me." The President ordered her and winked at me.

And this is how I became the President's tenth and final concubine.

The Richter Scale –
A Clavis on this Year
E.E. Rhodes

You have used this scale, measuring the destructions in your relationships, your job, your life. With specific events that are calamitous to an order of magnitude. And you've noted how often the potential for devastation occurs.

Where 1 is a microearthquake, not felt, or felt rarely. Recorded only by seismographs and those paying close attention. Almost continuous. Several million per year.

Where 2 is minor, felt slightly by a few people. With no damage to buildings or structures, except the chambers of the heart. And there are a million tremors over twelve months, and the average human heart beats thirty-five times that a year.

Where 3 is often felt, but rarely causes damage. Shaking of indoor objects may be noticed, in your workplace and home. Which may be the same thing now. Over

100,000 of these per year.

Where 4 is light, and there is a noticeable shaking of things indoors, accompanied by rattling noises. Felt by most people in the affected area. Slightly felt outside. Generally causes minimal damage. But you look at your family and know that it's already too much. Up to 15,000 per year.

Where 5 is moderate, and causes damage to poorly built structures, and you think about doctors, nurses, pharmacists and medical services. With slight damage to other infrastructure and what about schools and teachers too? Felt by everyone. Repeatedly. And there are 1,500 per year.

Where 6 is strong, and there's damage to well-built structures in populated areas. Your family. Yours. And even those who are resilient take some slight to moderate damage. And those who are weak are susceptible to worse. Felt in wider areas. Strong to violent epicentre shaking. And hellishly, hellishly, 150 times per year.

Where 7 is a major disaster. Causes damage to most structures: families; schools; work; lives. Where some will partially collapse or experience severe impact. And even those who are robust are likely to suffer trauma. Felt across great distances. More than one a month. Twenty times per year.

Where 8 is great. And there is major damage, structures likely to be destroyed. Will cause medium or heavy damage even to those who thought they were sturdy. Damaging across large areas. Felt through extended regions. Felt by everyone. One per year. But that is all of us. All of us. And you don't think you can take much more.

Where 9 is even greater. And there is near total destruction – severe impact or collapse of all structures and relationships. Heavy damage and shaking extends to distant locations. Beyond borders. Where aspects of life will never be the same again. And there will be permanent changes in ground and social topography.

Where 10 is off-the-scale. And about which there is almost silence. Where any survivors describe close-to-total destruction. And this unspeakable final number represents the once-in-a-lifetime utter dismantlement of our brittled, fragile lives. Because with fault lines and fractures, something once broken is eternally vulnerable, even when eventually restored or repaired.

The Blue Bay News: Local Charity Shocked
Karen Walker

Mom's train from Toronto was due at 10 p.m. It's late.

Good.

More time to pace the Blue Bay station, check out the others waiting here on this cold shoulder of a hill outside town. Do any of them know her? Will anyone recognise her?

More time to figure out what to say: *Hi, Mom.* That'd be fine. Friendly. *Merry Christmas.* Hope it will be. *Welcome home, Mom.* No, not that.

***

I haven't been to visit. My daughter went in June.

Her grandmother's new life was a shocker: the grubby walk-up with three locks on the door, all the macaroni and cheese and dry bread sandwiches, riding the subway because the car had been sold.

"Why?" Jess asked.

I told her what she already knew—"Money is tight for Gran,"—but not the dollars of it. That Mom, former treasurer of The Blue Bay Lighthouse Preservation Society, would be repaying $3350 per month for the next ten months.

***

I sweated in the dim, cold hallway outside the courtroom. Mom chatted with her lawyer, a cluster of lights overhead.

The glare slid down her pink silk blouse, bounced off her tight white skirt, pierced her grey frizzle to the roots, but didn't reveal what in the hell she was thinking.

She smiled and laughed, though the judge's ruling was ten minutes away.

***

Mom left Lucky behind. '*Not fair to take him to the city,*' read the tearjerker note I found on my kitchen table.

The snappy, ratty Pomeranian is ten and has as many teeth. Another is rotten. Here we are at the vet.

Mrs. Seymour, the lighthouse society's chairwoman, sits across the waiting room with a spaniel. Her dog has sympathetic, forgiving eyes, and we nod, smile at each other. Mrs. Seymour and Lucky exchange growls.

***

Mom's house has been for sale since spring.

The pool turned green in July—greener than the lawn—and the pretty maple in the front yard fell during a summer storm. Her roses, prickly and perhaps in denial, never bloomed for the buyers who came to look.

December's snow is a dusting of sugar on hard times. The ten-year-old next door to Mom's shovels the walk and the driveway. His mother now waves to me when there's no one around, even spoke when I dropped off a holiday card with his pay.

***

She's doing the quiz she had refused to do, the quiz I had emailed over and over.

Christmas tree lights blink on and off in her glasses.

"Here you go," Mom says, as if it's a gift.

She's answered three of the questions: ticked, flicked the 'yes' boxes beside 'Do I neglect responsibilities or abuse trust?' and beside 'Do I ignore how my behaviour affects others?', but slashed a big X into the 'no' of number ten—'Can I control my gambling?'

Ten Fingers

Amy Barnes

My mother's car slides under a semi-truck that piggy-backs it as glass falls on her face and the

truck falls on her pelvis and I curse Lana Turner for not living long enough to outfit the truck

that's just outside the retrofitting requirements, a truck that snuck out with no bar driven by a

truck driver that snuck out of the bar full of bottom shelf, bottom bar booze to drive his truck

with no bar like he's a drama star on prime time that can drink all he wants because it's not real

booze, just amber-tinted water in a glass.

Ten Things They Tell Me That I Know Not to be True

Marie Little

10. Everybody feels like this sometimes.

(I feel this lie in my belly like a pain. My mother attempts to hold my hand.)

9. We love you.

(This lie floats, like a fatty turd. It bobs up now and again, especially when you are already face-down in the mud.)

8. You know I don't mean it.

(The easiest, weakest of lies. Like burning the toast or forgetting milk.)

7. Your mother can't help it.

(A lie which tastes like soap. My father squirms.)

6. When you are older, you'll understand.

(A special lie for the young, which makes it worse; a lie you can't argue with. A powerful lie.)

5. Mummy needs it.

(A particular breed of lie, the kind that grows like mould in my father.)

4. We know you love us really.

(A risky lie. They tell this one through the medium of forced tears and after careful study of people with emotions.)

3. You will feel better in the morning.

(A lie based on lies. A domino-lie, to topple all others. They make eye contact with each other, but not with me.)

2. It helps me cope.

(An indigestible lie.)

1. I'm trying.

(A lie that also belongs to me.)

High School Reunion – 10th Year Edition
Kimberley Shiel

INSTRUCTIONS
Number of Players:
100 – 175 former classmates, teachers, and significant others

Equipment:
- The 1990 black satin prom dress that you never got to wear, altered
- A purse-size bottle of vodka
- Pack of tissues

Object:

To catch up with old friends and flaunt how happy and successful you are.

Set-up:

Lose ten pounds and silence your negative self-talk.

Play:

1. Have your mother drive your new 2000 Lexus SUV when she drops you off at your old high school.
2. Smile when the Biology teacher welcomes you and wonder if your stomach is churning from the scent memory of formaldehyde-soaked frogs or your nerves.
3. Exhale your nervous breath when you see Ms. Andrews. No one understands the complexities of a fallen woman more than an English teacher. You imagine her smoker's voice reading your life story to a new crop of high school students, as she used to read the stories of Tess and Hester.
4. Wave at your old high-school boyfriend and his wife – your old best friend. No need to say more. You've arranged to meet up with him before you leave town.
5. Scan the crowd for your other old friend Lisa. She always had your back.
6. During the banquet in the cafeteria, tell Geena the Gossip that that you are now an emergency room nurse and will be marrying a doctor in three weeks. Word will spread fast.
7. When you go to the gymnasium for the social evening, focus on how the garland, balloons and

twinkle lights have magically transformed the damp, rubber-smelling room. Try not to look at the stage.

8. You look at the stage and remember how difficult it was to climb the stairs. Your father wanted a picture of you accepting your diploma in a cap and gown. The heavy, blue graduation gown concealed your large belly, but everyone knew your "situation" and appropriately distanced themselves from you. You'd be pushing your son out before the photographs arrived by mail.

9. Act gracefully when your ex-boyfriend and ex-best friend are voted Cutest Couple, as many eyes will be on you. He never suffered for his indiscretion as you did, but you want to keep things pleasant with your son's father.

10. Excuse yourself to the washroom and sip the vodka. Raise your feet above the stall when The Two Jennifer's enter and start gossiping about you like the old days: *"I heard Sara is marrying a doctor twenty-years older than her."* The other Jennifer blurts out that her marriage is over and bursts into tears. You reveal yourself and pass her your pack of tissues, knowing intimately how tears just melt away the one-ply school toilet tissue.

The Winner:

A mature, self-confident person will say that there are no winners or losers, that everyone is just trying to live their best life. You survived public-shaming, alienation, and sexism to become a successful woman, yet still refuse to kick another woman when she is down. Relish in your victory.

Ten Stories Down
Noah Evan Wilson

By the time Adam is falling it no longer matters whether it was an accident, whether he was pushed, or pushed himself. All that matters now are the ten stories rushing toward him and the ground.

How strange, Adam thinks, that he has time to think *how strange,* let alone watch his reflection in that first window: grey flecks in his beard, his unzipped jacket fluttering like a sail. He is back on his solo sailing trip around the Gulf of St. Lawrence, same beard, and wind. It is the moment the wind starts up again, after days of idle floating, depression. He has no clothes on, screaming into the blue, longing to bottle up the feeling for when he returns.

Adam's body relaxes, spinning like the bottle that summer at camp; his stomach feels the same. He eyes Alice, tracking Thom in his periphery. The bottle stops, pointing between them. Alice leans across and pecks him on the lips before he has the chance to choose.

Fully upside-down, he hangs in his college room-mate's car that he has flipped on the highway. The taste of blood and alcohol on his lips will stay with him, though he will never drink again.

A passing bird becomes Adam's graduation cap falling toward him. Feeling as if he is suddenly suspended mid-air, he scans the crowd for his father who he knows isn't there. It's just a habit now.

Halfway down is the worst day of his life, the day he loses his temper at his partner, Javier, screaming at him as he trips down the stairs. Still yelling about a missed dinner reservation, he notices Javi lying at the bottom, no longer yelling back. *Is he breathing?* The thought is wordless, all-consuming. He is rushing down the stairs, rushing, rushing—

Javi waking up in the hospital. Adam realizes a face can be a complete story too in the moment it wakes, witnesses, forgives with the rise of a cheek.

Adam falls. The adoption falls through. They burn years of paperwork on the beach, have sex in the orange glow. Adam is gentle, mindful of Javi's injuries. They talk about *getting away*. Adam decides to sail alone.

Before he takes off, a letter arrives from his father. Adam carries it in his breast pocket around the gulf. It grows heavy, wet with rain, the letters appear to cry for them both.

Stories should have an arc, Adam learns not in school

but from his father, playing with toys on the worn carpet. He's a child again and his dad does all the voices, indulges every silly idea, ties up every loose end. He watches his dad, most alive acting out the beginnings.

This story is a straight line. Adam looks up from the end. It is the final chapter of his fall. All he ever needed was gravity, he considers, watching the replay. If only he could have lived so fully in each story before, he wonders, would he be

We Ate the Ice Cream First
Connie Boland

Ten days. Stranded in an elementary school.

Two hundred and forty hours. We invent games and silly songs to muffle the snowstorm screaming against brick walls. Snowbanks climb windows, blocking murky daylight.

Fourteen thousand, four hundred minutes. The principal glides from student to student. "Sleepovers are fun, aren't they?"

Eight hundred, sixty-four thousand seconds. In the north, we read the clouds, the horizon, the pre-storm silence. The November blizzard howls like a mortally injured polar bear. It buried our snowmobiles. Obliterated the playground.

We eat rainbow popsicles before the lights go out.

The first night, there was a panicked search for blankets and teddy bears, flashlights, and candles. Fifty kids in the library. Children with thumbs to their lips, snuggled together like storybooks on shelves. Teachers lay on grimy gym mats with flowery patterns.

"I was a student when this happened before," Jesse whispered. "Ten days…"

We draw pictures with broken crayons. Use magnetic letters to write six-word stories. In the gymnasium, Jesse snipped ten-foot lengths from a roll of thick brown wrapping paper, rusty scissors scraping the waxed hardwood floor. He told the kids to find a partner and trace each other.

"How are you holding up?" A decade ago, a class of 10-year-olds were outdoors when a ferocious blizzard rolled through our town. Three boys had dug a cave in a snowbank and were overlooked in the rush to get everyone back inside the school. The cave collapsed. Jesse's younger brother suffocated.

"I need to take a walk." I follow him, as silent as a shadow. In the bowels of the frigid building the music room is decorated with silver clefts and golden trebles. My best friend paces, corner to corner, up and over the risers. The room smells like dust, mouldy bread, and chalk. It reeks of loneliness.

A youngster with flushed cheeks, runny nose, and a chocolate milkstache hesitates at the door. "I miss my cat."

"What's your cat's name," I ask.

"Puddin'."

I tell the kid I miss my cat too. "Maybe they can be

friends when we go home."

"Maybe." He wanders away, an enormous, orange winter parka scratching the gritty floor.

"I have to get out of here," Jesse says. The school is ten kilometres down a dirt road. His fingers twitch against denim thighs. "I feel like I'm drowning." His hand is ice cold. I match his stride. Ten steps between corners.

"You couldn't save him."

"I knew they were out there. I should have made someone listen."

Ten hours later, no one has seen Jesse.

The little boy finds me on the eleventh day, huddled in a grey wool blanket, on the top riser. He wiggles with excitement. Wears a grin so wide it crumbles his milk-stache. "They're coming."

We burst into a third-floor classroom. Scrape frost from a window. Breathe on the crystals. Snowplows, banana yellow against stark white, lead a motorcade. A bumblebee bus with warning lights flashing red. Jesse sitting shot gun.

At Christmas in Your Fifties, There's a Lot of Time to Kill

Jason Jackson

Let's play a game.

I hate games.

A game about the number ten.

What do I have to do?

I ask questions. You answer them.

And how do I win?

You don't. But you don't lose either.

Weird game.

The best kind.

Come on then.

Ok, question one: What's the tenth step of the twelve?

Seriously? You're starting with that?

Answer the question.

You know I know this. Bloody hell.

Just answer...

It's the personal inventory one. Admitting you're wrong. Honesty. Humility. Reflection.

Very good.

Thanks. I love being patronised while playing a game I don't want to play.

Question two: The tenth commandment?

Adultery, right? This is a game with an agenda. We start with my drinking and now we're onto...

It's '*Thou shalt not steal*'.

Oh.

Oh, indeed.

So, no agenda?

No agenda. Just a game.

Next question, then.

Question three: According to Paul Simon, there are fifty ways to leave your lover...

Ah! I know this one. There aren't fifty. And there isn't a tenth. He only lists like, seven or eight. I used to be able to sing the whole thing...

Trick question. Well done. Two out of three.

And you're sure there's no agenda? Alcoholism, adultery, leaving your lover?

You're just paranoid.

If I get more than half-right, do we get to go to bed and, you know...?

It's half-three in the afternoon.

Oh yeah. We're too old for the spontaneous-sex-in-the-daytime thing.

Ok, well, let's say seven out of ten.

Ha! You're on! Next question.

Question four: for a tenth wedding anniversary, you should buy…?

I have absolutely no idea.

Worth a guess?

Well, paper's one. Gold's like, twenty-five or something. Ten's got to be something weird. Jade, or aluminium or…

Lucky bastard!

What? How?

Aluminium. Or tin. Either-or, apparently.

And what did I actually buy you on our tenth anniversary?

Nothing.

Oh.

We went to the dog track. You lost three grand.

Next question.

Okay. Question 5: tenth sign of the zodiac. A clue: it's mine.

Oh, I don't believe in that nonsense.

You don't believe in anything.

Yes I do. A higher power. The second step. The one everyone has an issue with.

And your higher power is…

You know what it is.

I know, but I like to hear you say it.

(brief pause): *Love.*

Say it again.

(longer pause)*: Love.*

(even longer pause): Ok. Enough questions. You won. Let's go to bed.

But I thought I had to get seven out of ten?

Three out of four's good enough for now.

But I didn't even get your star sign right.

I don't believe in that nonsense either.

But you said, 'it's three o'clock in the afternoon!'

Bloody hell! It's Christmas, isn't it? A girl's allowed to change her mind.

Yes, ok. But can I say something first?

You're in danger of spoiling the moment…

I just wanted to wish you a Happy Christmas.

Ok. Happy Christmas. Now, are you coming to bed, or do we have to finish the stupid game?

Author Biographies

Rosie Garland

Rosie Garland writes long and short fiction, poetry and sings with post-punk band The March Violets. Her latest collection *What Girls Do In The Dark* was shortlisted for the Polari Prize 2021. Val McDermid has named her one of the most compelling LGBT+ writers in the UK today. http://www.rosiegarland.com/

Sara Hills

Sara Hills is the author of the flash collection *The Evolution of Birds*. Her work has featured in the Wigleaf Top 50, SmokeLong Quarterly, Cheap Pop, X-R-A-Y Literary, Cease Cows, Fractured Lit, Flash Frog, and others. Originally from the Sonoran Desert, Sara lives in Warwickshire, UK and tweets from @sarahillswrites.

Jan Kaneen

Jan Kaneen started writing at the age of 50 as therapy to help channel her emotions. She now has an MA in Creative Writing from the Open University and her stories have won prizes hither and yon. She's been nominated for Pushcarts each year between 2016-2021.

Her memoir-in-flash, *The Naming of Bones*, is Available from Retreat West Books.

Monica Dickson

Monica Dickson writes short fiction. Her work has appeared in Splonk, jmww, X-R-A-Y and elsewhere. She's been long and shortlisted for various competitions and her story, Receipts, made the inaugural BIFFY50 list. She won the 2019 Northern Short Story Festival Flash Fiction Slam and is a 2021 graduate of the NSSF Academy. More at writingandthelike.wordpress.com and @Mon_Dickson.

Amanda Saint

Amanda Saint is the author of two novels, *As If I Were A River* (2016) and *Remember Tomorrow* (2019). Her flash fictions and short stories have been widely published in journals and anthologies and listed and placed in many competitions, including the Mslexia Flash Fiction Prize, Flash500, V300, and the Fish Flash Fiction Prize. She is currently writing a novella and a flash fiction collection. Amanda is the founder of Retreat West.

Gaynor Jones

Gaynor Jones is the recipient of a Northern Writer's Award and has won or been placed in competitions including the Bridport Prize, Bath Flash Fiction and the Mairtín Crawford Award. Her novella-in-flash Among

These Animals was published in March 2021. She is represented by Laura Williams at Greene & Heaton.

Amanda Huggins

Amanda Huggins is the author of the novellas *Crossing the Lines* and *All Our Squandered Beauty*, plus four collections of short stories and poetry. She has won numerous prizes for her travel writing and fiction, including two Saboteur Awards. She was also the first author to be signed by Retreat West Books!

Jude Higgins

Jude Higgins' flash fiction pamphlet *The Chemist House* was published by V.press in 2017 and her flash fictions are widely published in magazines and anthologies. She founded Bath Flash Fiction Award and directs the short short fiction press, AdHoc Fiction and Flash fiction Festivals, U.K. @judehwriter.

Christine Collinson

Christine Collinson writes historical short fiction and has just completed her first Novella-in-Flash. Her work has been published in a variety of online literary journals and print anthologies. She's been longlisted several times for her flash fiction, including in the Bath Flash Fiction Award.

Michael Loveday

Michael Loveday is a fiction writer and poet. His hybrid novella-in-flash *Three Men on the Edge* (V. Press, 2018) was shortlisted for the 2019 Saboteur Best Novella Award. His craft guide, *Unlocking the Novella-in-Flash*, is published by Ad Hoc Fiction in 2022. More at:
https://michaelloveday.com/
and
https://novella-in-flash.com/

Martha Lane

Martha Lane is a writer by the sea. Her stories have been published by Northern Gravy, Perhappened, Reflex Press, and Ellipsis Zine among others. Her novella about grief and sharks is due to be published by Leamington Books. Balancing too many projects at once is her natural state. Tweets @poor_and_clean.

Matt Kendrick

Matt Kendrick is a writer, editor and creative writing tutor based in the East Midlands, UK. His short fiction has been published in Bath Flash Fiction, Cheap Pop, Craft Literary, Fictive Dream, FlashBack Fiction, New Flash Fiction Review, Reflex Fiction, and elsewhere.

Rebecca Field

Rebecca Field lives and writes in Derbyshire, UK. She has work in several print anthologies and has also been published online by Reflex Press, The Daily Drunk, The Phare, Ghost Parachute, The Cabinet of Heed and Ellipsis Zine among others. Tweets at @RebeccaFwrites.

Ruth Brandt

Ruth Brandt's short stories and flash fiction have been widely published. She won the Kingston University MFA Creative Writing Prize, has been nominated for awards including the Pushcart Prize. Her prize-winning short story collection *No One has any Intention of Building a Wall* was published by Fly on the Wall Press in November 2021.

Mandira Pattnaik

Mandira Pattnaik is a writer and columnist. Pushcart Prize, Best of the Net and Best Microfictions-nominated, her short-form fiction appears or is forthcoming in Passages North, Best Small Fictions Anthology, DASH, AAWW and McNeese Review, among others. More about her can be found in
mandirapattnaik.wordpress.com.

Natalia Snider

Natalia Snider lives in the Rocky Mountains with her husband and pup. She is a creative working as a photographer, author, and artist. Currently, Natalia is pursing another degree in Creative Writing coupled with International Studies at the University of Colorado Denver.

Chris Cottom

Chris Cottom is a retired insurance copywriter (Key Features of the Stakeholder Transfer Plan) now trying to write other fiction: flash, novellas-in-flash, and short stories. Previous convictions include Harrods handbag seller and Christmas hamper packer. In the early 1970s he lived next door to JRR Tolkien.

Philip Charter

Philip Charter is a writing coach who works with non-native speakers. He is the author of two short-fiction collections, and his debut novella-in-flash, *Fifteen Brief Moments in Time*, is forthcoming with V Press in 2022. *The Fisherwoman*, the title story from Philip's second collection, was nominated for the Pushcart Prize.

Ian O'Brien

Ian O'Brien is a writer trapped in a teacher's briefcase. In

2020 he was shortlisted for the Cambridge Prize for Flash Fiction and his Novelette-in-Flash, *What The Fox Brings in Its Jaw*, is out now with Retreat West. He lives in the Welsh valleys. You can find him on Twitter @OB1Ian.

F.J. Morris

FJ Morris is an award-winning author and Director of the Oxford Flash Fiction Prize. Her collection *This is (not about) David Bowie* received a special mention in the Saboteur Awards for Best Short Story Collection 2019. In 2021, she was awarded Arts Council funding for her novel, *Burning down the house*.

Edward Barnfield

Edward Barnfield is a writer and researcher living in the Middle East. His stories have appeared in Ellipsis Zine, Lunate, Strands, Janus Literary, Leicester Writes, Cranked Anvil, and Reflex Press, among others. In 2021, he won the Exeter Literary Festival and Bay Tales short story prizes. He's on Twitter at @edbarnfield.

Tom O'Brien

Tom's latest Novella-in-Flash, *One for The River*, is out now from Ad Hoc. His debut *Straw Gods* was published by Reflex Press, and his Novelette-in-Flash, *Homemade Weather*, with Retreat West. Pushcart and Best Micro-fiction nominated, he's the winner of the 2021 NFFD

NZ Best Microfiction and the 2021 BIFFY50 Micro-fiction. He's on twitter @tomwrote and his website is tomobrien.co.uk.

Judy Darley

Judy Darley can't stop writing about the fallibilities of the human mind. Her fiction and non-fiction has been published in the UK, US, New Zealand, Canada and India. Judy is the author of short fiction collections *Sky Light Rain* (Valley Press) and *Remember Me to the Bees* (Tangent Books). Her third collection, *The Stairs are a Snowcapped Mountain*, will be published by Reflex Press in March 2022. You can find Judy at www.skylightrain.com.

Reshma Ruia

Reshma Ruia has written two novels, *Something Black in the Lentil Soup* and *A Mouthful of Silence*, shortlisted for the SI Leeds literary award. It will be published in June 2022 as *Still Lives*. Her poetry collection, *A Dinner Party in the Home Counties*, won the 2019 Debut Word Masala Award. Her short story collection, *Mrs Pinto Drives to Happiness* is out now. She is the co-founder of The Whole Kahani – a writers' collective of British South Asian writers.
www.reshmaruia.com

E.E. Rhodes

E. E. Rhodes is an archaeologist who lives in Wiltshire and Wales. Her prose and poetry is widely published in a range of anthologies and journals. She's one of the Friday Flashing team for Retreat West and facilitates creative nonfiction workshops as part of the Crow Collective.

Karen Walker

Karen writes short fiction and prose poetry in a basement in Ontario, Canada. Her work is in Reflex Fiction, Bullshit Lit, Sundial Magazine, The Disappointed Housewife, Retreat West, Potato Soup Journal, Unstamatic, Five Minute Lit, 100 Word Story, The Ekphrastic Review, and others. She tweets at @MeKawalker883.

Amy Barnes

Amy Cipolla Barnes writes short stories, flash fiction, CNF and essays for a range of sites. She's an associate editor at Fractured Lit, editor for Ruby Lit, co-editor at Gone Lawn and a reader for Narratively, CRAFT, and The MacGuffin. Her full-length collection Ambrotypes is forthcoming from word west in March 2022.

Marie Little

Marie Little lives near fields and writes in the shed. She has short fiction featured in: The Birdseed, Re-Side, The

Cabinet of Heed, Gastropoda, Free Flash Fiction and more. She also writes poetry (children's poetry as Attie Lime). Twitter @jamsaucer. www.marielittlewords.co.uk for more.

Kimberley Shiel

Kimberley Shiel lives in Winnipeg, Canada with her husband and a mischievous cat. She is an accountant who enjoys adding words together to create short fiction. In 2021, she began sharing her stories and soon made a few longlists. She placed second in the November 2021 Retreat West Micro Fiction competition.

Noah Evan Wilson

Noah Evan Wilson is a writer and musician based in New York City. His story, *The Fading*, won second prize in the 2021 Prime Number Magazine Flash Fiction Contest, and his latest record, *The View from the Ground* – EP, is now available on all major streaming platforms.

Connie Boland

Connie Boland (@BolandC) is an award-winning journalist, instructor, and communications professional in Corner Brook, Newfoundland and Labrador, Canada. In a cluttered basement bedroom, Connie tests the waters as a creative writer, and admits it's as challenging as navigating menopause. Her work is published in regional, provincial, and national publications.

Jason Jackson

Jason Jackson's prize-winning fiction appears regularly in print and online. His stories have been nominated for the Pushcart Prize as well as appearing regularly in the BIFFY 50 and Best Microfictions. Jason is also a photographer, and his prose/photography piece *The Unit* is published by A3 Press. Jason co-edits the online magazine Janus Literary.